she dreams of
Sable Island

a Paper Doll Book

Briana Corr Scott

NIMBUS
PUBLISHING LTD.
NIMBUS.CA

Nimbus Publishing Limited
3660 Strawberry Hill Street, Halifax, NS, B3K 5A9
(902) 455-4286 nimbus.ca

Printed and bound in China

NB1405

Editor: Whitney Moran
Design: Heather Bryan

Library and Archives Canada Cataloguing in Publication

Title: She dreams of Sable Island : a paper doll book / Briana Corr Scott.
Other titles: Sable Island
Names: Scott, Briana Corr, 1981- author, illustrator.
Description: A poem.
Identifiers: Canadiana 20189068280 | ISBN 9781771086264 (hardcover)
Subjects: LCSH: Sable Island (N.S.)—Juvenile poetry.
Classification: LCC PS8637.C6833 S54 2019 | DDC jC811/.6—dc23

Nimbus Publishing acknowledges the financial support for its publishing activities from the Government of Canada, the Canada Council for the Arts, and from the Province of Nova Scotia. We are pleased to work in partnership with the Province of Nova Scotia to develop and promote our creative industries for the benefit of all Nova Scotians.

Canada

Canada Council   Conseil des arts
for the Arts   du Canada

NOVA SCOTIA

To my little dreamers,
Izzy, Teddy, and Jo

She dreams of Sable Island
     She goes there in her sleep
The fog comes softly to her
     and she drifts across the deep.

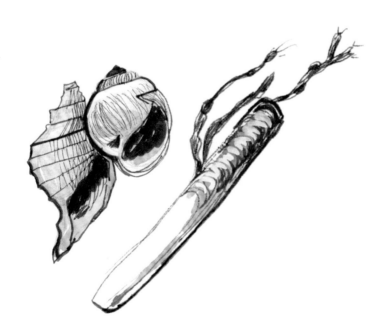

The island is a crescent
At last it comes in view
A moon eclipsed by ocean
White sands against dark blue.

Horses come to greet her

    As she stands on mounds of sand

Where nature lives unguarded
Where creatures rule the land.

She spends her time exploring
    Scales dunes and never rests
The island's voice is calling
    From flowers, shells, and nests.

The air is filled with tern calls
Wild horses graze nearby

Seals lounge along the shoreline
– Emerald sea and yellow sky

She visits all the shipwrecks
Stranded there by tides

She peeks in buried buildings
Covered window-high.

When hunger takes her over
She rests upon the sand

The island brings her oysters
A feast in her own hand.

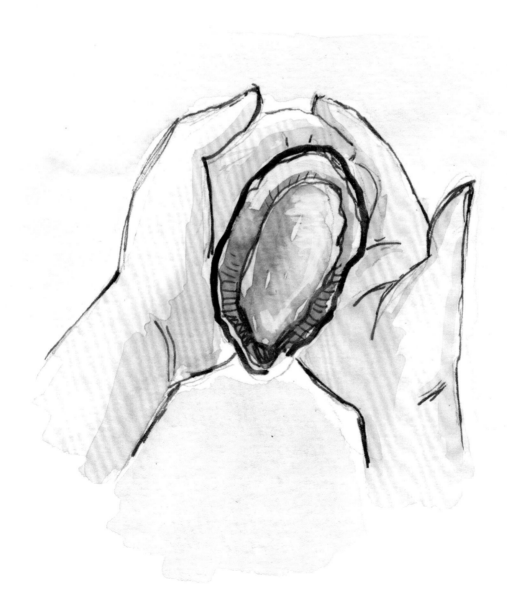

At last the sun is fading
  Fog sweeps her back to bed
With the song of Sable Island
  Still singing in her head.

About Sable Island

Sable Island is a real place, although it sounds like a dream. Located over one hundred kilometres south of Nova Scotia, in the Atlantic Ocean, the remote national park, protected by Parks Canada, is home to one of the largest grey seal colonies in the world, herds of wild horses, and many species of birds and plants. It is known around the world for its dangerous coast and the hundreds of ships that have wrecked there.

Not many people visit Sable Island, because it is hard to get there. (The only place to land a plane is on the beach!) It is an important place for scientists to visit and study weather

patterns and wildlife, and anyone else who visits is asked to take great care to not disturb the island's fragile habitats. (In this book, the dreamer is shown touching the horses and seals. Real visitors must keep their distance from all the creatures, so that the animals stay wild and the visitors are safe.)

Some animals and insects that live on Sable Island are found nowhere else. It is a wild place where humans have had little lasting influence. Many artists, photographers, composers, and poets have been inspired by the beauty and mystery of Sable and have made art about this wild sand dune in the Atlantic.

Plants and Animals of Sable Island

Grey seals and harbour seals live on Sable Island. In the winter months they come on shore to have their pups. Sable is home to the largest grey seal colony in the world.

Some flowering plants include wild rose, blue flag Iris, and cow lilies.

Blue Flag Iris

Cow Lily

Harbour Seal and Grey Seal

Arctic terns are very protective of their nests, which they make in grassy areas on the ground.

Ipswich Sparrow

Arctic Tern

Juniper

Sable Island horses are are believed to have been brought to the island in the mid-1800s by a Boston merchant.

The only breeding ground in the world for the Ipswich Sparrow is Sable Island..

White Marked Tussock Moth

Sable Island Horses

Various mushrooms grow out of the dung left by the horses, and these little gardens can be seen all over Sable Island.

There are a few species that live only on Sable Island, including a type of white marked tussock moth.

Mushrooms

Moon snails and surf clams are sometimes found on Sable's beaches. Moon snails prey on clams and other mollusks by boring holes into their shells.

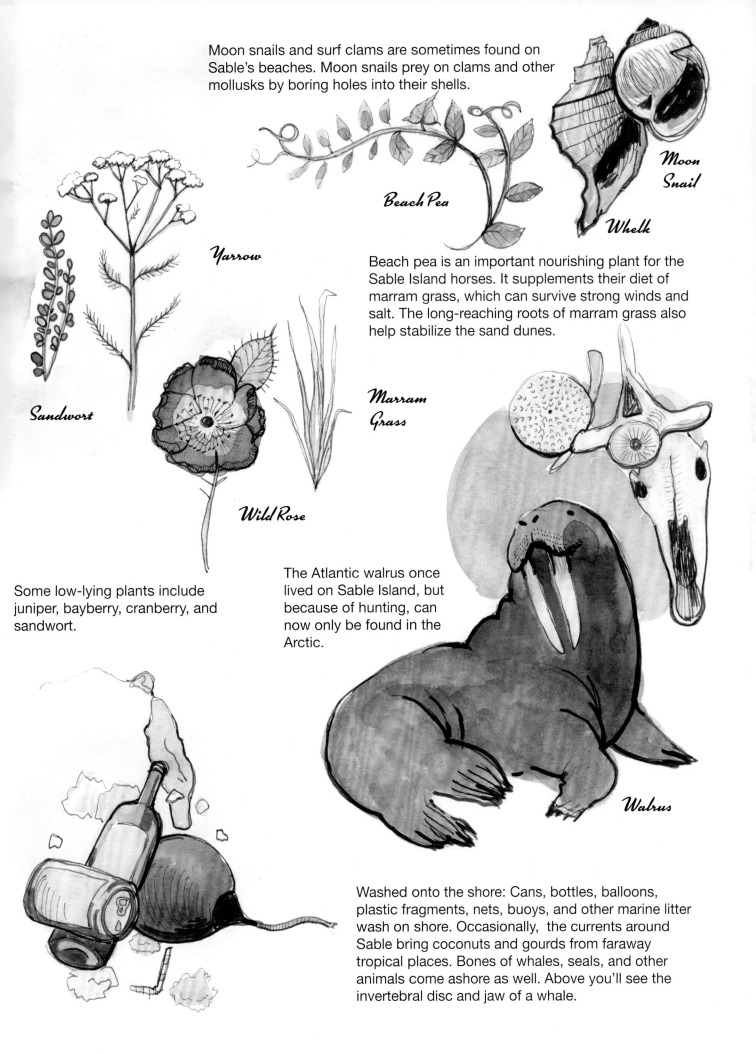

Moon Snail

Whelk

Beach Pea

Yarrow

Sandwort

Wild Rose

Marram Grass

Beach pea is an important nourishing plant for the Sable Island horses. It supplements their diet of marram grass, which can survive strong winds and salt. The long-reaching roots of marram grass also help stabilize the sand dunes.

Some low-lying plants include juniper, bayberry, cranberry, and sandwort.

The Atlantic walrus once lived on Sable Island, but because of hunting, can now only be found in the Arctic.

Walrus

Washed onto the shore: Cans, bottles, balloons, plastic fragments, nets, buoys, and other marine litter wash on shore. Occasionally, the currents around Sable bring coconuts and gourds from faraway tropical places. Bones of whales, seals, and other animals come ashore as well. Above you'll see the invertebral disc and jaw of a whale.